Mermaid School

The Clamshell Show

The
Mermaid
School
Series

Mermaid School

The Clamshell Show

Look out for more in the series—coming soon!

Mermaid

School

The Clamshell Show

Written By

Lucy Courtenay

Illustrated By Sheena Dempsey

Amulet Books
New York

Library of Congress Cataloging-in-Publication Data

Names: Courtenay, Lucy, author. | Dempsey, Sheena, illustrator.
Title: The Clamshell Show / Lucy Courtenay ; illustrated by Sheena Dempsey.
Description: New York : Amulet Books, 2020. | Audience: Ages 6 to 9. |
Summary: Marnie competes against her friend Orla and Gilly, a new student at Lady Sealia Foam's Mermaid School, for the lead role of Queen Maretta in the annual Clamshell Show. Identifiers: LCCN 2019057746 | ISBN 9781419745201 (hardcover) | ISBN 9781419745218 (paperback) | ISBN 9781683359296 (ebook) Subjects: CYAC: Musicals--Fiction. | Theater--Fiction. | Mermaids--Fiction.| Schools--Fiction. Classification: LCC PZ7.1.C6813 Cl 2020 | DDC [Fic]--dc23
LC record available at https://lccn.loc.gov/2019057746

Hardcover ISBN 978-1-4197-4520-1
Paperback ISBN 978-1-4197-4521-8

Text copyright © 2020 Lucy Courtenay
Illustrations copyright © 2020 Sheena Dempsey

Printed and bound in U.S.A.
10 9 8 7 6 5 4 3 2 1

Amulet Books are available at special discounts when purchased in quantity for premiums and promotions as well as fundraising or educational use. Special editions can also be created to specification. For details, contact specialsales@abramsbooks.com or the address below.

Amulet Books® is a registered trademark of Harry N. Abrams, Inc.

ABRAMS The Art of Books
195 Broadway, New York, NY 10007
abramsbooks.com

For
Mary Foley.
S.D.

Chapter One

Marnie Blue and her friends, Orla Finnegan and Pearl Cockle, were waiting beside a large rocky bulletin board outside Lady Sealia's office. Marnie covered a yawn. It was early. Much earlier than they usually came to school. But auditions for the Clamshell Show only happened once a year, and Marnie had been too excited to sleep in.

Marnie's aunt Christabel, Mermaid Lagoon's most famous radio star, had gotten her first big break at the Clamshell Show. Now it might be Marnie's turn. She couldn't wait. The lights! The music! The famous guests in the audience, the music agents, and the record producers! Marnie had been practicing her singing exercises for *weeks*.

The only thing missing was the audition sign-up sheet.

"It should be up by now," whispered Orla. "They *said* it would go up this morning. Why is it taking so long?"

Marnie checked the large starfish clock that clung to the wall above the headmistress's door for what felt like the hundredth time. It had hardly moved.

"I guess we just have to wait," she whispered back. "And we'd better keep our voices down." Lady Sealia was not someone who liked to be disturbed.

Orla glanced at the small freckled mermaid beside her. "Why are you here, Pearl?" she asked. "This audition sheet is for the singing parts."

Pearl Cockle's singing voice was well-known at Lady Sealia's Mermaid School. And not for any good reasons.

"I'm not here to audition," Pearl said, flicking her golden tail. "I just got up early so I could do some fish-spotting. And then I saw you guys, so I followed you into school." Her eyes shone. "I spotted a luminous carnival fish this morning. They only come out at dawn, and they are SUPER rare."

"Boring," said Orla.

"You promised never to be mean to Pearl again," Marnie reminded Orla. "Not since she helped rescue you from the East Lagoon Rocks—"

Orla blew her dark hair out of her eyes. "Sorry," she sighed. "You're right." Then she folded her arms and glared at the wall, as if she could change the time with the power of her mind.

"Although I am going to be in the show," Pearl added. "I'm playing the rock tuba in the orchestra."

"Really? Don't you have to audition?" asked Marnie.

"I'm the only rock-tuba player in the school," Pearl explained. "So I've definitely got the part."

Rock-tuba players were rare, Marnie knew that. Rock tubas were rare too. There were only two in the whole of Mermaid Lagoon: one in the school Music Cave and a huge one in Clamshell Grotto, where the show took place.

 3

"Aunt Christabel says the rock tuba in Clamshell Grotto is so powerful that if you blow the low notes too hard, the whole place falls down," said Marnie.

Orla's dark eyes widened. "Seriously?"

"Aunt Christabel is full of stories," Marnie admitted. "I never know what to believe."

"I'll avoid the low buttons anyway," said Pearl with a giggle. "Just in case."

Marnie felt a ripple in the current. More mermaids were arriving. They swam straight up to the bulletin board, pushing Marnie and the others out of the way as they tried to find the sheet for the Clamshell Show auditions. The water churned and swirled.

"Where is it?"

"Where can I put my name?"

"I'm going to audition for the lead!"

"The sheet isn't up yet," Marnie tried to tell them.

But no one was listening. Marnie was jostled around, and pushed into the wall. Pearl and Orla disappeared underneath a pile of multicolored tails. Marnie fought her way to the top of the pile, and waved her arms, trying to get everyone's attention.

"The list isn't up yet," she shouted, as loudly as she could. "IT'S NOT UUUUUUP!"

Suddenly, Lady Sealia's door burst open. Marnie froze at the sight of the tall, silver-haired headmistress. All the other mermaids fell silent.

"Who is shouting outside my door?" Lady Sealia demanded. "You've woken up Dilys."

Lying in Lady Sealia's arms, Dilys the dogfish blinked sleepily at Marnie. Marnie's heart sank. She knew what was coming.

"Marnie Blue." Lady Sealia fixed Marnie with her icy stare. "I've said all along that you are a troublemaker. Just like your aunt!"

Marnie felt her cheeks turning red. Having a famous aunt caused a LOT of problems. Aunt Christabel had been a troublemaker at school, and a few of Marnie's teachers thought Marnie was the same way. But she wasn't. It was very unfair.

"Dilys does NOT appreciate noise at this time in the morning," Lady Sealia said. "And neither do I."

"Yes, Lady Sealia," said Marnie, squirming. "Sorry, Lady Sealia. Sorry, Dilys."

Dilys had already gone back to sleep.

"Make way!" cried a voice. "Make way please!"

Marnie heard the clank of a heavy coral necklace. The music teacher Miss Tangle came shooting toward them. Octopuses swim backward, so Miss Tangle bounced off the walls a few times before she stopped beside the bulletin board.

"Good morning everyone!" Miss Tangle gurgled. "Good morning, Lady Sealia! Good morning, Dilys!"

The music teacher tickled Dilys under the chin with a tentacle. Her other tentacles put the audition sheet on the bulletin board and stuck it in place with several barnacles. Everyone rushed forward again.

Marnie realized that she hadn't brought a pen to add her name to the list. As she opened her mouth to

ask Orla if she could borrow hers, Lady Sealia gave her another hard stare. Marnie suddenly had a horrible feeling that the headmistress was going to punish her. Maybe even stop her from auditioning. She would DIE if she couldn't audition. Why, oh WHY was she related to Christabel Blue?

"Please take it from here, Miss Tangle," said Lady Sealia. She stroked Dilys's head with her long pale fingers. "Dilys needs her beauty sleep."

"Of course, Lady Sealia!"

The headmistress's study door swung shut.

"Come along now!" said Miss Tangle, clapping her tentacles as Marnie breathed a sigh of relief. "Sign-up time for singers! The orchestra sign-up is this afternoon," she added, looking a little anxiously at Pearl.

"I know, Miss Tangle," said Pearl. "Don't worry, I wasn't going to sing."

"Thank Neptune for that," muttered Miss Tangle. "Well now!" she continued, looking at the rest of the mermaids. "Who would like a chance to sing in this year's Clamshell Show? There are solo parts, duets, and places in the chorus."

A sea of hands waved brightly colored shell pens.

"Me, Miss Tangle!"

"I want to, Miss Tangle!"

Marnie studied the audition sheet eagerly.

CLAMSHELL SHOW

Lady Sealia's Mermaid School and
Lord Foam's Atoll Academy present the
Annual Extravaganza of the Seas:
Queen Maretta and the Storm Sprites.
A well-known tale of courage,
drama, and friendship.
Auditions are NEXT WEEK!

Marnie almost squeaked with joy. *Queen Maretta and the Storm Sprites* was her favorite. The story was exciting and romantic. The songs were amazing and she could sing them all by heart. She knew what part she wanted to play.

"I'm going to audition for Queen Maretta," Orla said, scribbling her name on the sheet. "What about you, Marnie?"

Marnie felt a little surge of worry. She should have known this would happen.

"I'm going to audition for Queen Maretta too," she said, a bit nervously.

Orla laughed. "Come on! Everyone knows Queen Maretta had dark hair." She pushed back her long inky-black locks and looked meaningfully at Marnie's silver-blonde head.

"Miss Tangle won't give the part to you just because your hair is dark," Marnie said, as bravely as she could.

"I know that," Orla replied. "Miss Tangle will give it to me because I'm the best singer in the school."

Marnie's confidence wobbled. Miss Tangle liked Orla more than she liked Marnie. Marnie thought it was because Miss Tangle had taught Aunt Christabel long ago and had never recovered from it. And Marnie did have to admit that Orla had an amazing voice, rich and dark like stormy midnight waves. Marnie's voice was more like the surface of the lagoon on a summer's day: bright and clear and sparkly. Which was best for Queen Maretta?

Marnie told herself not to give up so easily. "You're not the best singer in the school," she told Orla. "You're just *one* of the best."

Orla looked disbelieving. "You're really going to audition for Queen Maretta?"

Marnie clasped her hands so that they didn't shake. She hated arguing, especially with her friends. "Yes," she said.

"Well, I guess you can do what you want," Orla said with a shrug.

Marnie felt awash with relief. "Great," she said, and tried to smile. "Can I borrow your pen so I can put my name down? I forgot mine."

Orla held out her purple shell pen for Marnie. But as Marnie reached to take it, Orla let go. The pen sank beneath the beating tails of all the mermaids signing up for the auditions, and vanished from sight.

"Sorry," said Orla.

But she didn't sound sorry at all.

Chapter Two

"I'm sure it's nothing to worry about," Marnie's mom said at dinner a few days later.

Marnie prodded her clam risotto around her shell bowl. "Orla hasn't talked to me all week," she said gloomily. "And she avoids me at lunchtime."

"Friends are the worst," said Aunt Christabel.

Marnie's aunt was sitting next to Marnie at the dinner table, wearing a large pair of pink coral sunglasses that covered most of her face. She folded up the letter she was reading and put it in her bag. Her pet goldfish, Garbo, was swimming in circles above their heads, annoying Horace the anglerfish as he dangled his light over the table.

"I'm sure you don't mean that, Chrissie," said Marnie's mom.

Aunt Christabel picked up her spoon and took a

large mouthful of clam risotto. "I don't mean ALL the time," she said, chewing. "I just mean SOME of the time. Many of my worst fights have been with my best friends."

Marnie's lip wobbled. "But I don't want to fight with her," she said.

"You used to fight all the time," Aunt Christabel reminded her. "At the beginning of the year, you two couldn't stand each other!"

"Yes, but that was ages ago. We've been friends ever since Pearl and I found her when she went missing." Marnie didn't mention that they had rescued Orla from the East Lagoon Rocks. That area was out of bounds and very dangerous, and Mom would be furious if she found out.

Aunt Christabel pointed her spoon at Marnie. "You know what the answer is, don't you?"

Marnie shook her head.

"Don't audition for the part of Queen Maretta."

Marnie almost dropped her spoon. "But I WANT to audition!" she said indignantly. "I want to play the Queen! I've been practicing all of the songs, I've been doing all of the singing exercises you taught me, and I really think I'd make a good Queen Maretta."

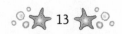 13

"Quite right, darling," Marnie's mom said. "I'm not sure you're helping, Chrissie."

Overhead, Garbo darted past Horace. Horace snapped irritably, sending shadows scurrying across the cave walls.

"Stop teasing Horace, Garbo," Christabel scolded. "You know he can't catch you."

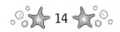

She took off her sunglasses and dangled them by one coral arm. "I *am* helping, Daffy. I'm showing Marnie that she wants the part of Queen Maretta more than Orla Finnegan's friendship."

"But I want both!" Marnie exclaimed.

"Sometimes you have to choose between a friend and a career."

Something in Christabel's voice made Marnie look up. To her surprise, her aunt's eyes looked a bit red and puffy. Had she been crying?

Christabel slid her sunglasses over her eyes again. "I have to go," she said, rising from the table and picking up her bag. "Come along, Garbo. My Big Blue Show won't make itself."

And she swept out of the kitchen with Garbo beside her.

"I've never seen my aunt cry before," Marnie told Pearl as they swam to school the next day. "Her eyes were bright red."

Pearl's own eyes turned misty. "Maybe she was crying about her true love."

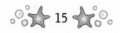

15

Marnie sighed. "Not this again, Pearl. I honestly don't think Aunt Christabel has a true love," she said.

"We all saw her crystal tears that day in the Radio SeaWave studio," Pearl insisted. "Everyone knows that mermaids only weep crystal tears for their true love. And remember the words we found carved near the East Lagoon Rocks when we rescued Orla? *Christabel loves Arthur*. There's only one Christabel I know in this lagoon, and Arthur's her true love, whoever he is. I just know it."

"But she's never mentioned anyone named Arthur," Marnie objected, "and we don't know anyone with that name."

"Then it's a tragic true love," said Pearl in triumph. "That's the best kind."

"Maybe she was just allergic to Mom's clam risotto," Marnie suggested. "Oh, Pearl, what am I going to do about Orla? She's definitely ignoring me and sulking. I *want* to stay friends with her, but I need to do this audition."

"That's your answer," said Pearl. "You *want* to stay friends, but you *need* to audition. *Need* always wins."

Marnie didn't think it was as simple as that.

"It's only the first audition," Pearl added. "Maybe neither of you will get the part of Queen Maretta. Come on, or we're going to be late."

There weren't many seats left in the large Assembly Cave at the top of School Rock. Marnie looked around uneasily. There were a LOT of mermaids waiting to audition. How many of them wanted the part of Queen Maretta? Maybe Pearl was right. Maybe neither she nor Orla would get it.

"We will go in groups," said Miss Tangle when the school scallops had flapped back to the main office with the registers. "Dora Agua, Mabel Anemone, Lupita Barracuda, Marnie Blue? You're up first."

Dora Agua looked worried. She raised her hand. "Miss Tangle?" she said. "Can we audition in private?"

"If you can't audition in front of an audience, you'll never be able to sing on the Clamshell Stage, Dora," said Miss Tangle. She beckoned with all eight of her tentacles. "Don't dawdle now."

Marnie checked her tail, which she'd polished especially for today's auditions, and swallowed her nerves. Every eye in the Assembly Cave followed Dora, Mabel, Lupita, and Marnie as they swam on to the stage. Even Lady Sealia's portraits on the rocky walls seemed to be watching. Marnie snuck a glance at Orla, who was sitting near the front. She tried her hardest not to mind when Orla looked away.

"You've all learned the audition piece?" asked Miss Tangle.

Marnie had been singing the songs from *Queen Maretta and the Storm Sprites* for years with her aunt. She knew the audition piece so well that it had been creeping into her dreams all week. She nodded with the others.

"Then away we go!" said Miss Tangle, lifting her tentacles. "You'll each sing a verse. Marnie, you can start."

"Over the water, over the blue," Marnie sang.

"Traveling far away from you,
Into the dark where the storm sprites fly,
Wishing you could stay close by . . ."

The song was about Queen Maretta leaving her love, Prince Cobalt, and going to war with the storm sprites without knowing if she'd ever come back. It was so sad and beautiful that Marnie could feel her eyes pricking with tears.

If Aunt Christabel really had been thinking about her tragic true love at dinner, no wonder her eyes had been puffy.

"Lovely!" exclaimed Miss Tangle when all four mermaids had sung. "Apart from you, Lupita dear. You were flat."

Lupita sighed.

"You can be in the chorus," said Miss Tangle kindly.

"There may be some extra spaces. Dora, you were a little off-key too. I think it might be best if you worked in stage management. Marnie and Mabel? Good work. I'll see you at the second auditions this afternoon."

"Well done!" Pearl said enthusiastically as Marnie swam back to her seat with her mind in a whirl. "You were great!"

Marnie's head was still spinning as Miss Tangle took the next group of mermaids through the tune. She didn't have the part yet, but she didn't **NOT** have the part either. All she had to do was sing her best in this afternoon's second auditions and maybe she would be Queen Maretta! She pictured the Clamshell Stage with its beautiful set, and all the musicians in the Seaharmonic Orchestra, and all the agents and record producers and friends and family listening to her. She wondered dreamily which of the merboys from Atoll Academy would play Prince Cobalt.

"Psst," Pearl hissed at her. "It's Orla's turn."

Marnie snapped to attention. Orla was on the stage with Finnula Gritt, Kerri Kelp-Matthews, and someone she'd never seen before. She stared at the unknown mermaid's cloudy golden hair and upturned nose. Who was she?

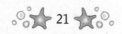

"From the top, please!" said Miss Tangle.

Orla sang really well. Marnie had to admit that. She started worrying again. If Orla got the part, how was she  going to feel? Marnie didn't want to be a sore loser. She didn't want to be a loser at all! This whole thing was giving her tail-ache.

Now the new girl had started singing. She was really good too. Her voice wasn't as deep as Orla's. It was lighter and softer, more like Marnie's.

"Orla and Gilly, see you this afternoon for second auditions," Miss Tangle trilled. "Finnula and Kerri, we need some mussel-drummers. I think that's where your talents might lie. The orchestra auditions are after lunch."

The next four auditions got underway. Orla swam over to Marnie and Pearl, grinning.

"Well done," said Marnie, trying to smile.

"Thanks," said Orla. "You were good too."

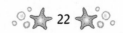

"Wait," Marnie blurted out as Orla turned to go. "Do you want to have lunch together?"

Orla turned back. "You want this part, right?"

Marnie bit her lip and nodded.

Orla shrugged. "Well, I want it too. I think it's best if we stay out of each other's way until Miss Tangle makes a decision."

Marnie worried she was going to cry. "Fine," she said, doing her best not to let her voice wobble. "And whatever Miss Tangle decides, we both accept it."

"Shake on it," Orla said.

They shook tails. Pearl watched them both with a frown.

"Ellie Plankton, Salmonella Stone, Treasure Jones, and Jaya Wetson please!" Miss Tangle sang out from the stage.

Marnie let go of Orla's tail.

"May the best mermaid win," she said, trying to be fair.

Orla tossed her long dark hair. "Don't worry. She will."

Chapter Three

Marnie sat on a rocky seat at the back of the Music Cave, swinging her tail as she waited for Pearl to finish with the Seaharmonic Orchestra. She could smell the scent of starfish fingers wafting up from the Dining Cave, and she was hungry. Normally she would have gone to lunch with Orla, but since Orla didn't want to, she was waiting for Pearl instead.

Although Pearl wasn't auditioning, Miss Tangle had asked her to play the rock tuba—a huge spiral of stone studded with limpet buttons—to accompany the auditioning mermaids and get in a bit of practice before the rehearsals. A few strands of red hair floating around the sides of the stone instrument was the only proof that Pearl was behind the rock tuba at all.

"No no no!" shouted Miss Tangle as one of the younger mermaids played a wrong note on her coral clarinet.

"One last time from the top, the middle, and the bottom. Pearl, can you hear me?"

The answering blast from the rock tuba made all the music stands wobble. Miss Tangle waved a few driftwood batons at the sea-glass violins, coral clarinets, sea-urchin ocarinas, bladder-wrack bagpipes, cuttlefish kazoos, and mussel drums, and the music started up again. Marnie leaned against the rock wall and tried to ignore her

rumbling tummy. At this rate, there wouldn't be any starfish fingers left. And she still had to check the time for the second round of auditions this afternoon.

"Louder with those mussel drums, Kerri and Finnula!" cried Miss Tangle with enthusiasm. "More from the sea-glass violins! We really do need a razor-clam flute player. I hope Atoll Academy has one."

There was a burst of chatter among the mermaids.

The merboys at Atoll Academy were always an interesting topic of conversation, and the Clamshell Show was one of the only times the two schools got to meet. Marnie found it a bit annoying how giggly some of the mermaids got when the merboys were mentioned.

Pearl gave one final thunderous blast on the rock tuba as Miss Tangle produced a seaweed handkerchief and mopped her forehead.

"That will do for now," she said. "You've all made it through this audition. Congratulations. The Seaharmonic Orchestra will meet for our first rehearsal next week."

There were a few claps and cheers.

"Will the boys from Atoll Academy be there, Miss Tangle?" asked Finnula Gritt. Kerri Kelp-Matthews giggled.

"I certainly hope so," said Miss Tangle.

Pearl swam out of the rock tuba's stone coils. "Where are the rehearsals going to be?" she asked, a little breathlessly.

"In Clamshell Grotto, of course," said Miss Tangle. Gasps of excitement rippled around the room. "We must get used to the new acoustics!"

"I can't believe I'm going to play the Clamshell Grotto rock tuba next week!" Pearl said as she and Marnie swam as fast as they could to the Dining Cave. "Apparently it's ten times bigger than the school one. I haven't been this excited since I spotted an albino catfish."

Marnie looked anxiously at the starfish clock above the door of the Dining Cave. What time was the second round of auditions? Miss Tangle had said they were this afternoon, but when? It was already almost a quarter past. Would she have time for lunch? She was starving.

Suddenly there was a flash of purple tail and the gleam of a pearl necklace as Orla swam past with Mabel. Just as Marnie was wondering whether to ask her about the audition times, Orla turned around.

"Our audition time this afternoon has changed. It's at half past, not quarter past," she said. "I thought you should know."

Marnie felt a stab of relief. She would have time for starfish fingers after all!

"Thanks!" she called as Orla and Mabel vanished around the corner. The faint sound of Mabel's laughter floated back down the corridor toward her.

Marnie joined Pearl in the lunch line, humming "Over the Water."

"Marnie?" said Pearl.

Marnie heaped starfish fingers on to her plate and scooped up a heap of sea-cucumber salad. "What?"

Pearl scrunched up her freckled face. "I think Mabel and Orla are up to something."

Marnie carried her plate of food to a table. "What do you mean?" she asked as she gobbled down her first starfish finger. Auditioning made her hungry.

"I don't know," Pearl admitted. "But—"

"Marnie Blue?"

Marnie swung round. Ms. Mullet, the crab deputy head of Lady Sealia's, was swimming past with a starfish-finger sandwich in her claws.

"Shouldn't you be heading for your audition?" said Ms. Mullet. "Your name is on Miss Tangle's list, I believe."

Marnie tried to swallow her food and answer at the same time. "It's at half past, Ms. Mullet," came out as "Harf parf, Miff Muwwef!"

Ms. Mullet's sharp eyes bobbed on their stalks. "I

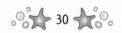

think you will find Miss Tangle is taking your auditions at a quarter past," she said. She waved her claw at the wall. "It's spelled out very clearly on that bulletin board and it's very unprofessional for a performer to be late."

The deputy head scuttled on through the Dining Cave. Marnie gaped at the large notice barnacled beside the doorway. She hadn't noticed it on the way in.

CLAMSHELL SHOW
SECOND ROUND OF AUDITIONS:
Ellie Plankton, Salmonella Stone,
Gilly Seaflower, Jaya Wetson
Five past the afternoon starfish
Treasure Jones, Marnie Blue,
Orla Finnegan, Mabel Anemone
Quarter past the afternoon starfish
Music Cave
DO NOT BE LATE!

Marnie couldn't believe her eyes. Quarter past? But that was . . . *now*.

"I told you Orla and Mabel were up to something," said Pearl.

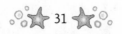

Marnie crammed the rest of her lunch into her mouth as fast as she could. Orla had lied. May the best mermaid win, indeed!

"Come on, Pearl." Marnie shoved herself away from the table and thrashed her tail against the current. "Orla isn't getting away with this."

"What about my lunch?"

"Bring it with you!"

The Dining Cave was right at the bottom of School Rock, under the seabed itself. Marnie fought her way through the crowds, swimming up the rocky tunnels back to the Music Cave. She should have stayed there after the Seaharmonic Orchestra auditions, she realized. Lunch could have waited.

"Excuse me!" she cried as she battled through the mermaids surging through the corridors. "Can everyone get out of the way please? Swimming late for an audition! Thank you . . . Thanks . . ."

Past the stables. Through the Sports Caves, dodging the mermaids playing fishball in the high nets. Past the library—quietly, to avoid annoying Len the venomous lionfish librarian. Marnie beat her tail as hard as she could as she swam up through the Oceanography Cave and past the practice rooms. Her breath was coming in short gasps. The words *I'm going to be late, I'm going to be late, I'm going to be late* drummed through her head on an awful loop. Miss Tangle wouldn't listen as she tried to explain what had happened. Miss Tangle would give the part to Orla . . .

Waiting outside the Music Cave, Orla and Mabel jumped as Marnie came pelting around the corner. Marnie swam up to Orla and poked her hard in the chest. Pearl floated anxiously in the background.

"You cheated!" Marnie gasped.

"You should have gotten to the Dining Cave in time," Orla said defensively. "Then you would have seen the notice for yourself."

"I thought we were going to play fair!"

Orla looked sulky. "You said 'may the best mermaid win.' Well, maybe the best mermaid just plans ahead."

Marnie had never felt so upset in her life. "If you're going to cheat, then I don't want to be friends with you anymore!"

Orla turned bright red. "Well, maybe I don't care!"

"What in Neptune's name is this awful racket?"

Miss Tangle appeared at the door of the Music Cave with her tentacles folded across her chest.

Marnie pushed Orla out of the way. "I'm here for my Queen Maretta audition, Miss Tangle!"

Orla pushed Marnie back. "So am I, Miss Tangle!"

"Don't worry Miss Tangle," Pearl said, finishing her starfish fingers. "I'm just here to watch."

"I suppose you want to be Queen Maretta too, Mabel?" Miss Tangle said, looking at Mabel Anemone.

Mabel blushed. "I want to be a storm sprite, actually."

Miss Tangle nodded. "Come on in then," she said. "I'm still looking for storm sprites."

"But Miss Tangle—" Marnie began.

"But Miss Tangle—" said Orla.

"What about Queen Maretta?" they said at the same time.

Miss Tangle looked over her glasses at them. "I'm sorry, girls, but I've already found my Queen Maretta," she said.

The new mermaid with the golden, cloud-like hair and the upturned nose swam out of the Music Cave. She grinned at Orla and Marnie.

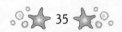 35

"This is Gilly Seaflower," said Miss Tangle. "Such a voice! Such a talent! Gilly is going to make a marvelous Queen Maretta. I can feel it in my suckers!"

Just then Treasure Jones swam round the corner, panting loudly.

"Did I miss it?" she asked.

Chapter
Four

Marnie, Orla, and Pearl shut themselves in a practice room to recover from the shock.

"Who the flippering flatfish is Gilly Seaflower?" said Orla.

"She speaks fluent Octopus and has a brother at Atoll Academy," said Pearl.

"How do you know that?" said Marnie in surprise.

"Because I listen during the morning assembly," said Pearl. "She started yesterday."

Orla thrashed her tail. "Who speaks fluent Octopus? I bet that's why Miss Tangle gave her the part." She reached for Marnie's hand. "I'm really sorry about the way I've acted, Marnie. I was horrible to you."

Marnie felt giddy with relief. "You were," she agreed. "But I forgive you."

"You're too nice to be my friend," Orla said. She looked embarrassed. "I wouldn't forgive me."

"I know," Marnie said. Orla laughed.

"At least we can play storm sprites in the show," Marnie added. "They're good parts and we'll still be on the Clamshell Stage. So that means hopefully there will be some record producers and agents listening to us."

Orla stuck out her bottom lip. "I don't WANT to be a storm sprite."

Marnie didn't want to be a storm sprite either. The storm sprites were the bad guys. The storm sprites would wear horrible costumes, and everyone would boo them. She sighed as she thought about the beautiful costumes that Gilly Seaflower would wear and the lovely songs she was going to sing.

"It's not fair," growled Orla.

"You promised you'd accept Miss Tangle's decision," Pearl reminded Orla. "You and Marnie even shook tails on it."

Miss Tangle pushed open the practice room door. She peered at Orla, Marnie, and Pearl. "You three should be in your art class by now," she said. "Can you take Gilly with you? She's new and isn't sure where the art studio is. I'm sure you'll look after her."

Orla gave Gilly a dirty look and swam away with a flip of her purple tail.

"Poor Orla always struggles with defeat," said Miss Tangle. "Now, I can offer you a little extra practice after school, Gilly. Queen Maretta has a **LOT** of music to learn."

"I don't need any extra practice, Miss Tangle," said Gilly.

Marnie thought that was pretty rude.

Miss Tangle blinked. "OK then," she said. "We're meeting outside the Oceanography Cave next week and swimming in formation to Clamshell Grotto for the first rehearsal. It's all going to be wonderful, so make sure you

know all your words by then, practice some of those dance moves I've just shown you, and give me a shout if you need any help."

The octopus teacher swam away, humming to herself. At least someone was happy, Marnie thought gloomily. Her mom had always taught her to be polite, so she did her best to give Gilly a welcoming smile.

"Hi, I'm Marnie," she said.

"I'm Gilly," said Gilly, crinkling her green-gold eyes. "In case you haven't figured that out."

"I'm Pearl," Pearl added.

Gilly ignored Pearl and studied Marnie. "Everyone says you're Christabel Blue's niece," she said. "Is that true?"

Marnie felt her cheeks flush. "Yes."

Gilly linked her arm through Marnie's. "That's so cool. I think she's amazing. Can I meet her?"

"I'm Pearl," said Pearl a little louder.

"Whatever," Gilly said, glancing at Pearl without interest. "Can we be friends, Marnie? Please say yes."

"Sure," Marnie said uncertainly. "You can sit with me and Pearl in art if you want."

Gilly clapped. "That would be off the reef! And can we go meet your aunt after school?"

"I don't know—" Marnie began.

"She'll enjoy meeting me," said Gilly confidently. "I'm going to be a star one day. She'll probably want to interview me. Oh, and can I bring my brother?"

"Um," said Marnie. "I don't—"

"Great!" Gilly sang. "You're the best! Whoops, we'd better get to art. Is it this way?"

And she tugged Marnie down the hall, leaving Pearl to catch up.

"Gilly Seaflower is horrible," Orla announced as Pearl and Marnie joined her in the hall after art class. "Did you hear her in there? She was all, 'Oh, the art at my old school was SO much better' and 'I can draw stonefish in my sleep.' Urgh!"

Gilly had sung throughout most of the class, and at one point she swam up to the ceiling to perform a verse of "Over the Water." The class had gone wild. Everyone loved it. Even Ms. Mullet, who was the substitute that afternoon, had cracked a smile.

"Gilly's pretty full of herself," Pearl said. "But you have to admit that she's an amazing singer."

"She's not **THAT** amazing," Orla muttered.

Marnie didn't know what to think. Gilly had been really nice to her in art, telling her jokes and complimenting her on her conch shell painting. But she'd also been rude about pretty much everyone else, whispering in Marnie's ear about Pearl's crooked teeth and Ms. Mullet's cracked old shell. That had made Marnie feel guilty.

"I think she's just trying to fit in," she said.

Orla snorted. "Gilly Seaflower doesn't want to **FIT IN**. She wants to **STAND OUT**. Someone needs to teach her a lesson."

"You can't be mean to her," said Marnie in dismay.

"Why not?" said Orla.

"Because she's new and it'll make us look like sore losers."

"Well maybe I *am* a sore loser," Orla said with a frown. "And besides, she's pretty mean herself. Don't think I didn't hear her whispering to you about Pearl and Ms. Mullet."

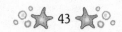

Pearl looked worried. "What did she say about me?"

"Nothing," said Marnie quickly.

"She said you look like a viperfish, Pearl," said Orla.

Pearl's eyes filled with tears, but she tried to laugh it off. Marnie felt awful.

"The only viperfish around here is Gilly Seaflower," said Orla.

"Did someone say my name?"

Gilly had come out of the art studio and was floating toward them. She gave Marnie a big smile. Feeling embarrassed and not wanting to be rude, Marnie smiled back. Orla made a disgusted sound, grabbed Pearl by the hand and pulled her away. Gilly didn't seem to notice.

"Hey!" Gilly's green-gold eyes were bright. "So we're going to meet your aunt at Radio SeaWave, right? I've always wanted to see inside a radio studio. I already sent my brother a scallop, telling him to meet us outside." She linked arms with Marnie again. "You'll love Jet. He's almost as talented as me. He's going to play Prince Cobalt in the Clamshell Show. When we drop in to your aunt's show, she's going to be so surprised!"

Marnie was starting to get a bad feeling about this.

"Don't you think Orla Finnegan is a perfect storm sprite?" Gilly asked with a giggle. "She looks mean enough to curdle seawater. But you're way too pretty to be a storm sprite, Marnie." Gilly patted her own golden curls. "If there were two Queen Marettas, you would definitely be the other one. It's a shame that it's only going to be me getting all the attention."

Marnie didn't know whether to smile or not. This was all very confusing.

"And thank Neptune that Pearl Cockle is only in the orchestra." Gilly burst out laughing. "I know she's your friend, but really! Her face would frighten off the storm sprites before the show even started."

Marnie didn't join in with Gilly's laughter. She realized then and there that she didn't want to go to Radio SeaWave with Gilly at all. Orla and Pearl were right: Gilly Seaflower was mean.

"Gilly," she began. "I don't think. . ."

But Gilly wasn't listening. She dragged Marnie toward a bored-looking merboy with flowing blond hair, who was waiting outside the Assembly Cave entrance with his arms crossed.

"Jet!" Gilly squealed. "You came! This is Marnie. She's going to introduce us to Christabel Blue."

Jet Seaflower looked at Marnie like she was a lump of seahorse poop. "Cool," he said.

Gilly was still holding Marnie's hand. "Radio SeaWave is this way, isn't it? This is going to be so much fun!"

Marnie didn't want to do this. Not at all. But she couldn't figure out how to get away. Gilly held her hand firmly. Almost as if she knew Marnie might try to escape.

Marnie worried the whole way to the Radio SeaWave
studio. What was Aunt Christabel going to say when she
showed up with Gilly and Jet? Her aunt didn't like people
dropping by without an invitation. She was working.
And she really didn't like show-offs.

"So I'm going to ask for loads of sparkles all over both
my dresses," Gilly trilled, fluffing out her hair as they
swam along the coral reef. "And I'm going to ask for two
more songs because five solos isn't enough. How many
are you going to ask for?"

"Dunno," said Jet. "The same I guess."

Gilly gasped with excitement at the driftwood sign
hanging beside a dark opening in a nearby rock: **RADIO
SEAWAVE THIS WAY.** She seized Jet's hand and swam
inside without waiting for Marnie. Marnie followed them
anxiously, through the rocky tunnel and into the studio.

Sam was working on the Radio SeaWave sound system with a pair of shell headphones clamped over his ears and his green-bearded chin resting on his hand. Orla's sister Sheela, the studio assistant, was polishing the window of the recording booth. Aunt Christabel herself was sitting at the long driftwood table that ran down one side of the studio, a shell pen in her hand. They all stared at the new arrivals in surprise.

"Is this it?" Gilly said, gazing around the studio. She was obviously disappointed. "It's really small. You don't even have any windows."

Christabel rose from the table. Garbo tumbled off her lap and opened her golden mouth in an *O* of annoyance.

"And who are you?" Christabel asked.

"Oh, Marnie invited us," said Gilly. "I'm Gilly, and that's my brother Jet. You haven't heard of us yet, but we're going to be famous. We'll come on your show if you want. We've got the lead parts in the Clamshell Show. You could do an interview with us. I'm going to be Queen Maretta and my brother will be Prince Cobalt."

Christabel gave Marnie a sympathetic look. She knew how much Marnie had wanted the part.

"Where's your VIM area?" Jet asked, looking around.

"VIM?" repeated Christabel.

Jet smoothed back his golden hair. "Very Important Merpeople. Obviously."

Marnie's face heated up with embarrassment. She gave her aunt a pleading look. *This isn't my fault*, she wanted to say. *They invited themselves.*

Aunt Christabel shot Marnie a wink. *I understand*, she seemed to say.

"Well," she said aloud. "We're very honored to have two budding stars in our humble studio. I'm Christabel. This is Sam, our sound engineer, and Sheela, our studio assistant."

51

Sam nodded. Sheela waved her polishing sponge. Gilly ignored them both.

"What's it like, being famous?" she asked Christabel eagerly.

Christabel's eyes glinted. "Hard work."

Gilly looked like she couldn't believe it. Jet laughed as if Christabel had said something stupid. Marnie squirmed hopelessly in the corner.

"Success isn't just about talent," said Christabel calmly. "It's about learning your craft. It's about teamwork, and sharing the credit. No one succeeds alone."

"Maybe you just don't have as much talent as us, then," Jet suggested, "if you need to rely on anyone else."

That was so incredibly rude that Marnie wanted to melt away on the spot. Sheela's mouth fell open and Aunt Christabel looked stunned.

Marnie fixed her eyes on the table so she didn't have to look at Gilly or Jet for one more second and saw that Aunt Christabel had been in the middle of writing a letter.

She didn't read more because Christabel was ushering Gilly and Jet toward the door. "It's been lovely to meet you both," Christabel was saying. "Do come again."

"You can contact our agent when we get one," said Gilly, fluffing up her cloudy curls. "After the Clamshell Show, we're going to be in high demand."

"You really should have a VIM area," Jet said.

Marnie was feeling embarrassed AND confused now. *Dearest Arthur, you know it's impossible . . .*

Aunt Christabel DID know someone named Arthur. And she called him *Dearest*. What was impossible? Perhaps Pearl had been right about this tragic true love thing after all.

"Well, that was fun," said Sheela sarcastically as Gilly and Jet swam away without even saying goodbye.

"I'm really sorry, Aunt Christabel," Marnie said. "It just sort of . . . happened."

Christabel's smile had something sharklike about it. "Don't be sorry, darling," she said. "I'm very interested to find out what happens to those two *charming* individuals. What a shame Miss Tangle gave that girl the part you wanted."

"I told you Gilly was awful," Orla said triumphantly the next day, as Marnie, Orla, and Pearl swam through the lagoon together. Brightly colored fish darted around them in the deep blue water. "I heard about what happened at Radio SeaWave from my sister last night. Sheela went on and on about how rude they were. Did Gilly's brother really say that he was more talented than Christabel?"

"Stay together, everyone!" Miss Tangle called, swimming at the head of the group. "Not far to Clamshell Grotto now!"

Marnie was desperate to talk to Pearl about the letter she'd seen on Aunt Christabel's table. But Pearl was fish-spotting, and she couldn't get her attention.

"I've never been to Clamshell Grotto," said Orla. "Is it as pretty as everyone says?"

Christabel had performed on the Clamshell Stage a few times, and Marnie and her mom had been in the audience. Just thinking about Mermaid Lagoon's most famous venue gave Marnie barnacle-bumps all over her skin.

"It's amazing! The stage is a huge sparkly clamshell, and the coral on the walls is every color you can think of," she said.

"Good thing I took my allergy pills this morning," Pearl chipped in. "Coral always makes me sneeze."

"The pearl-string curtains make this incredible tinkling sound when they lift them," Marnie went on. "And there are inlaid-shell seating boxes all around the sides so that everyone has a perfect view."

"A perfect view of Gilly Seaflower would be upside down in the school sea-cucumber patch," Orla said.

Marnie couldn't help laughing.

"Here we are!" Miss Tangle twittered. "Come along!"

Orla's jaw dropped. Pearl stopped counting striped blennies. This part of the lagoon was deep and the light was dim, but the Clamshell Grotto was unmissable. It was completely covered with colonies of phosphorescent fish, and glowed like a great underwater moon.

Inside, everything was even bigger and sparklier than Marnie remembered. The rock-crystal chandelier overhead dazzled with thousands of little fish, scattering silver spots of light around the walls. The seats in the stalls were lined with pale sea moss. The pearls in the curtains shimmered.

"Look," said Finnula Gritt. "Merboys!"

Several Atoll Academy merboys were sitting in the orchestra pit. A few others were messing around

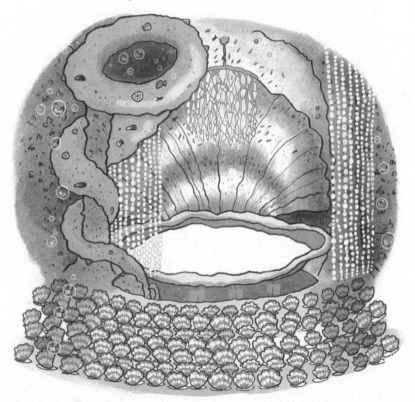

on the stage, daring each other to swim up to the huge rock-crystal chandelier.

"Come, come! Singers, on the stage!" called Miss Tangle, clapping all her arms together. "Orchestra players, in the pit! We have a lot to do today!"

Pearl stared at a looping stone structure that twisted up the multicolored coral walls. It wound among the shell-patterned seating boxes, and spiralled around one of the rocky columns that held up the roof, and opened its big stone mouth in the gloom high above the chandelier.

"Leaping lobsters," she said. "Is that the rock tuba?"

"I think it's the largest rock tuba in the world," said Marnie, squinting at it.

"No squidding," said Orla.

Miss Tangle zoomed toward the coral conductor's stand in a swirl of tentacles and tapped it with five or six batons. "Orchestra, take your seats! Storm sprites, stage left!"

The fish around the rock-crystal chandelier raced away to hide in their holes, dimming the lights. Pearl headed to the rock tuba. The mermaids and merboys in the Seaharmonic Orchestra tuned their instruments, and Orla and Marnie took up their positions on the stage with the other storm sprites.

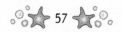

"Hi," said a cheery-looking merboy with a deep brown tail. "I'm Eddy. Are you storm sprites too?"

"Yes," said Marnie shyly.

Eddy grinned. "Nice to meet you. It's more fun being the bad guys, don't you think? I tried out for Prince Cobalt, practiced for hours, but Jet Seaflower got it."

"We tried out for Queen Maretta," said Marnie.

"Don't tell me," said Eddy. "Jet's sister got the part?"

Orla and Marnie nodded.

"I'm just the BEST singer in the WHOLE of Mermaid Lagoon," Eddy said, in a perfect imitation of Jet's bored voice. "And my sister is SO talented."

Marnie gave a startled giggle. She liked Eddy. "I'm Marnie and that's Orla," she said. Orla gave Eddy a wave. "Our friend Pearl is playing the rock tuba."

Eddy looked impressed. "My friend Algie is in the orchestra too. He plays the razor-clam flute."

Miss Tangle would be pleased, Marnie thought. She stared at the boy holding the unusual-looking flute down in the orchestra pit. Algie looked a bit like Pearl, with his swirling red hair.

"Queen Maretta?" shouted Miss Tangle over the noise of tuning clarinets, violins, and bladder-wrack bagpipes. "Where is my Queen Maretta?"

Gilly and Jet were nowhere to be seen.

"Maybe Gilly IS upside down in the sea-cucumber patch," said Orla.

Eddy looked interested. "Why? Did you put her there?"

"I wish," said Orla.

Miss Tangle looked at the huge starfish clock that clung above the door. "Well, we can't wait," she said, clearly annoyed. "Before we begin, there are just a few things we need to go over. There is only one exit in Clamshell Grotto. If there is an earthquake, a hurricane, or a typhoon, everyone is doomed. Any questions?"

The merpeople looked at each other a little anxiously. That didn't sound good.

Miss Tangle suddenly laughed. "Only joking!" she said. "There is another way out. But it's only ever used

in the face of absolute and total disaster, or discovery by humans. Lady Sealia did tell me . . . What was it now? I'd forget my suckers if they weren't part of my tentacles—"

The doors flew open.

"We're here!" trilled Gilly Seaflower, sweeping into the auditorium with Jet behind her.

Miss Tangle sighed with relief. "At last! Come on, quickly now! Seaharmonic Orchestra? Take it from the top, middle, and bottom!"

Chapter Six

The vibrations of the rock tuba shuddered through Marnie's scales. That was the storm sprites' cue. For about the tenth time that morning, she, Orla, Eddy, and the others swam onto the stage.

"Your scariest expressions now!" Miss Tangle cried. "I want to see ugly faces!"

Marnie pulled her best evil storm sprite face. She sang the angry, stomping words with the others. It was starting to come together now.

"WE are the storm sprites,
WE like to start fights,
WE stir the waves, OH!
WE drive the wind, OH!"

"Scarier!" shouted Miss Tangle. The rock tuba boomed. The bladder-wrack bagpipes blasted. "You're the villains! Be villainous!"

Eddy was right, Marnie thought as she scowled and punched the water with her fists in time with the others. *Playing the bad guys* is *kind of fun*.

"**WE** *are the storm sprites*," she sang, over and over again.

"WE like to WIN fights!
WE storm the shore, OH!
WE fight some more, OH!"

"**OW**!" shouted Orla as Lupita hit her by mistake.

"**OH**!" sang the storm sprites.

"**OOH**!" shouted Lupita as Orla hit her back.

Miss Tangle waved her batons. The orchestra fizzled out. "Chorus and orchestra, take a break," she said breathlessly. "Coral clarinets and razor-clam flute? Stay please. Gilly and Jet, on the stage now!"

Marnie swam over to join Pearl beside the rock tuba.

"I wish I could try out these low buttons," Pearl said wistfully, stroking a row of fat limpets on the tuba's stone coils. "But I don't want to knock everything down."

"I've got something to tell you," Marnie blurted.

"What?" asked Pearl, her eyes lighting up.

"It's about Aunt Christabel," said Marnie. "She was writing a letter yesterday, to 'Dearest Arthur.' I think you're right. She might have a true love!"

Pearl clapped her hands. "I knew it! What else did the letter say?"

Marnie screwed up her face, trying to remember. "'You know it's impossible,'" she said.

Pearl looked surprised. "It's not impossible. You just tell me."

"No." Marnie shook her head. "That's what the letter said. 'You know it's impossible.'"

"You know *what's* impossible?"

Marnie had been wondering the same thing. "Being together?" she guessed.

"Do hurry up, Gilly!" Miss Tangle called. "We don't have all day."

Marnie and Pearl looked over at the stage.

 63

"Just a minute!" Gilly was giggling about something with Jet in the auditorium. "Jet's telling me this REALLY funny story and—"

The octopus looked at Gilly and Jet over the top of her spectacles. "Now!"

Gilly tossed her golden curls but swam on to the stage. Jet followed.

"That's better," said Miss Tangle. "Let's take a look at 'Over the Water.'"

"Which one's that?" asked Jet.

Miss Tangle blinked. "The big song before Queen Maretta goes to war."

Jet scratched his head. "I'll probably recognize it when it starts."

Miss Tangle looked like she was going to say something. Then she sighed and lifted her batons. The coral clarinets played softly. Eddy's friend Algie's flute floated over the top. Marnie felt her stomach melt. The melody was so gorgeous and sweet. She wished with all her heart that she was the one singing it.

Twirling dreamily in the middle of the stage, Gilly missed her cue.

"Concentrate, Gilly!" cried Miss Tangle.

Gilly stopped twirling and folded her arms. "I don't know why we have to rehearse this. I know it already."

"When's my solo?" said Jet, who had swum up to admire his reflection in the glimmering rock-crystal chandelier.

Pearl leaned toward Marnie when Jet and Gilly eventually finished rehearsing the song. "They're pretty annoying, aren't they? You'd have been a much better Queen Maretta."

Marnie smiled. "Thanks, Pearl."

"But, Marnie, you have to ask your aunt who Arthur is," Pearl added.

"I can't," Marnie said. "It's private."

"Then we'll never know," said Pearl, with a dramatic sigh.

"Those selfish Seaflowers are getting Miss Tangle's tentacles in a twist," said Orla, swimming over with Eddy

and his friend Algie. "I knew she should have chosen one of us. What are you talking about, anyway?"

"Christabel Blue's true love," said Pearl.

"Shhhhh! I said it was private, Pearl," said Marnie hastily. "I don't think we should tell everyone."

"I'm not everyone," said Orla, looking offended. "And neither are Eddy and Algie."

"Hi," said Eddy. Algie waved.

Marnie sighed. "Fine. Pearl and I have found out that my aunt Christabel might have a true love named Arthur, but it's impossible for them to be together."

"Nothing's impossible," said Orla.

"It's impossible for a yellow-headed jawfish to eat when it's brooding eggs," said Algie.

Pearl looked interested. "Why?"

"Because it broods its eggs in its mouth," Algie explained.

Algie and Pearl chatted about fish while Orla braided her hair with a long piece of golden seaweed she had found. Marnie leaned against the coils of the rock tuba and hummed along to Jet and Gilly rehearsing their last big number "Always Be Friends." Christabel had sung "Always Be Friends" to Marnie when she was very young, and it was one of Marnie's favorites. Gilly's voice was really strong and clear, and Jet matched his sister perfectly note for note. The only problem was, they kept getting the words wrong.

"Oh dear," moaned Miss Tangle as Jet sang the wrong verse for the fourth time. "Perhaps we should leave that for now. Please practice it at home. But now, let's work on the dance moves for the grand finale instead. Chorus, back onstage please!"

The current swirled around the auditorium as the chorus and the storm sprites returned, waving their tails idly and whispering. Gilly and Jet swam to the front, where Gilly performed a few somersaults.

"Remember everyone," said Miss Tangle. "The storm sprites and the Queen are FRIENDS now. So no more scowling." She looked at Lupita and Orla. "Or punching."

"I thought the Queen and the sprite things were enemies," Jet said.

Miss Tangle wiped her forehead. "You've just been singing about friendship. Don't you know the story at all, Jet dear? After the fight scene, everyone agrees that storms can be useful for the ecology of the lagoon."

"I'm good at fighting," said Jet.

"Can we talk about my costume soon, Miss Tangle?" Gilly asked.

With a great clattering of coral stools, the orchestra settled down for the finale. Finnula and Kerri crashed out the rhythm on the mussel drums. The cast tried to go through their dance moves. Fins to the left, fins to the right, somersault, hold hands, and repeat. But Marnie squashed her tail and bumped noses with Eddy. Lupita bumped into Orla, on purpose this time. Orla jumped on Lupita. Everyone else jumped on Orla. There was a lot of shouting.

Miss Tangle waved her tentacles. "Gilly, stop dancing in front of everyone! Jet, come **DOWN** from the chandelier! Oh tails and scales, this year's Clamshell Show is going to be a *disaster*!"

Marnie concentrated as hard as she could, turning somersaults until she felt sick. Despite all the chaos onstage, Pearl's words floated around and around in her head: *You have to ask your aunt who Arthur is.* It couldn't hurt to ask, right? She would talk to her aunt at some point.

Bobbing around on the deck of his boat, Arthur Bagshot studied the nautical map with a large magnifying glass. He peered at a section of the lagoon off to the south-southeast. The water there was deep. Undisturbed. Anything could be down there.

Anything at all.

He had left a letter for Christabel at the East Lagoon Rocks, where they'd left each other messages in the old days. His heart had almost jumped out of his chest when the letter disappeared. Surely Christabel was the only one who could have found it.

But she hadn't written back.

Arthur had decided to take matters into his own hands. He was tired of waiting.

"Set a course for south-southeast," he called to the captain, folding up his map. "I'll tell you when to stop."

The captain put his head out of the engine room. "What are we looking for then, boss?" he said cheerfully. "Treasure?"

"Oh no," said Arthur. "Something even more precious than that."

Chapter Seven

"Can I come with you to the studio tonight, Aunt Christabel?" Marnie asked. "I want to talk to you about something."

Christabel gave Garbo the dirty bowl of seaweed soufflé for the little goldfish to suck at before placing it in the hot-vent dishwasher. "Of course you can, darling," she said. "I'm recording my advertisement for the Clamshell Show. You can come and give me some feedback."

"That's OK, isn't it, Mom?" Marnie asked. "If I go out with Aunt Christabel to the studio?"

Marnie's mom waved a hand vaguely in the air. "Don't be late back," she said. "Horace? Living room. I need to mend the hem on my best seaweed gown, and I can't see a thing without some overhead lighting."

Marnie's mom left the room with Horace dangling his light ahead of her. The kitchen grew dim.

"This all sounds very secretive," said Christabel. "What do you want to talk to me about? Is it about a boy?"

"Yes," said Marnie honestly.

Aunt Christabel found her blue sea-moss coat and clipped on Garbo's leash. "I'm not sure you're old enough for boys yet," she said, opening the door.

Marnie flushed. "Oh, it's not about me, Aunt Christabel. It's about . . . someone else."

"Someone older than you, I hope?" Christabel laughed.

Marnie nodded. And gulped. How DID you ask a grown-up about whether they'd ever been in love?

"It's you, Aunt Christabel," she blurted. "I want to ask about YOU and a boy."

Christabel looked sideways at her. "Oh no. You saw my letter in the studio. Didn't you?"

Marnie nodded. "I didn't mean to. And I saw the rock too. *Christabel loves Arthur.*"

Marnie had never seen her aunt look so shocked.

"When did you see that?" Christabel asked, pressing a hand to her heart. "Don't you know how dangerous it is to swim around the East Lagoon Rocks? Your mom would have a fit if she found out. There are humans near there, Marnie. Do you want us all to be discovered?"

"I've seen your crystal tears too," Marnie plunged on. "Pearl told me what they meant. Aunt Christabel, is Arthur your true love?"

Christabel sighed but didn't answer the question. "Flip and Sam are waiting," she said. "We ought to hurry."

Marnie didn't give up. "If he's your true love, why can't you be together?" she asked, swimming after her aunt.

"It's complicated."

Aunt Christabel swam up the rocky tunnel and into the little studio. Marnie followed.

"Hey Chrissie," said Sam. "Ready to record?"

Christabel's producer, Flip, grinned through his blue beard and handed Christabel a sheet of seagrass paper. Christabel read it through as Sheela swam over with a hot cup of kelp tea.

"Any thoughts on the wording of this ad for the Clamshell Show, Sheela?" asked Christabel, taking the tea.

"Maybe add something about 'soFISHtication'?" Sheela suggested.

Christabel laughed, and Flip grinned, his gold tooth flashing.

"Good one," called Sam.

Marnie thought about Aunt Christabel's words of advice for Gilly and Jet. *Success is about teamwork, and sharing the credit. No one succeeds alone.* Christabel, Sam, Flip, and Sheela were a great team.

Christabel swam into the recording booth, placed the shell headphones on her head and leaned in to the sea-sponge microphone. Sam flipped a switch to red, and Marnie heard her aunt's voice boom around the studio.

"Your annual opporTUNAty to enjoy a WHALE of an evening is back! Yes folks, it's CLAMSHELL SHOW time. The *Big Blue Show* will be broadcasting from Clamshell Grotto FOR ONE NIGHT ONLY, bringing you all the glamour and gossip. It'll be a night of star appeal and soFISHtication. What are you waiting for? Get your tickets today!"

"Great! Let's do one more take, to be on the safe side," said Flip. "Ready to go again, Chrissie?"

Sheela swam over to Marnie. Even though Sheela was Orla's sister, Marnie always felt shy around the

older mermaid with her short hair and ruby-colored tail. She was so cool and talented.

"How are the Show-off Twins?" Sheela asked.

"Still showing off," Marnie said. "They're always late to rehearsal, and they still don't know their lines."

Sheela's dark eyes glinted. "Someone needs to teach them a lesson. Don't you think?"

Before Marnie could answer, the recording light blinked off.

"Great work, Chrissie," Sam said into his microphone.

"We'll put the advertisement out on tomorrow's show," said Flip.

Christabel swam out of the booth, leaving the shell headphones on Sam's mixing desk. Marnie opened her mouth to ask about Arthur again. But Christabel patted her cheek before she could say a word.

"Enough questions, shrimp," she said.

And that, Marnie realized, was all her aunt was going to say.

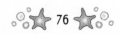

Chapter Eight

Marnie and Orla sat on the Clamshell Stage and waited for Miss Tangle to stop throwing her batons at the singers and the orchestra. Dress rehearsal wasn't going well.

"I'm sure everything will be fine," Marnie's mom had said brightly over breakfast that morning, as Marnie went through her dance moves with a piece of seaweed toast in one hand and a glass of sea-anemone juice in the other. "I believe in you all, and I can't wait to see the show tomorrow. Break a fin, darling!"

But then Marnie had spilled her juice on Horace the anglerfish mid-somersault and he'd switched his light off in a huff and she hadn't been able to find her school things in the dark and she'd ended up with a tardy from Ms. Mullet. She should have guessed right then that her mom's confidence wasn't going to be enough to get her through the day.

"You don't know your lines," Miss Tangle screeched at one of the storm sprites.

PING! A baton bounced off a mussel drum.

"You don't know your moves!" she shouted at the chorus.

THWANG! Another baton flew over Marnie's head and got stuck in the pearl curtains.

"You can't stay in tune. You're behind my beat," bellowed Miss Tangle at the sea-glass violins and bladder-wrack bagpipes.

DOINK! DOINK!

Down in the orchestra pit, Algie pulled a baton out of his razor-clam flute.

"The audience will **LEAVE** at the intermission and I will be served up as a salad on a record producer's plate!" Miss Tangle had run out of batons. She flailed her tentacles instead. "The show is tomorrow. **TOMORROW!**"

"Aunt Christabel always says a show gets worse before it gets better," Marnie whispered to Orla, doing her best to stay positive.

"Well, it's certainly gotten worse." Orla sighed. "Has your aunt said anything else about that Arthur guy yet?"

Marnie shook her head. She'd been trying to think of ways to get her aunt to talk to her about Arthur all week, but Aunt Christabel had made it clear the subject was off-limits.

"Jet and Gilly!" Miss Tangle wailed. "Why aren't my stars onstage? JET AND GILLY!"

Marnie glimpsed a cloud of golden hair high up in one of the seating boxes that lined the walls of the grotto. Gilly leaped out of the box and swam down to the stage. Jet swam after her, beating his dark blue tail lazily.

"What were you two doing up there?" Miss Tangle demanded. "Cast members shouldn't be in the boxes. The boxes are reserved for record producers, agents, and important members of the audience only."

Marnie saw a flash of blue out of the corner of her eye. She peered up at the box. Someone was there, just out of sight. She was sure of it.

"Jet and Gilly were just talking to someone up in that box," she hissed at Orla as the storm sprites gathered in their starting positions.

"Who cares?" Orla said. "I'm not interested in anything those idiots do."

The rock tuba blasted, making the chandelier shake.

"That's our cue," said Orla, grabbing Marnie's arm.

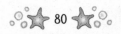

"Start singing, or Miss Tangle will throw something else at us."

Marnie tore her eyes away from the box high up on the rocky wall.

"WE are the storm sprites,
WE like to start fights,
WE stir the waves, OH!
WE drive the wind, OH!"

Gilly and Jet were now whispering together on the far side of the stage. They were up to something, Marnie could tell. But what?

Chapter
Nine

Marnie gazed at herself in the long rock-crystal mirror. It was the night of the show at last. OK, so her costume was grey and black. But at least the tiny iridescent shells sewn along the hem were sparkly. She leaned in closer to the mirror and rubbed white makeup into her cheeks. She drew big black circles around her eyes, and blinked at her reflection. A gruesome storm sprite blinked back.

"You look awful," said Orla. She'd backcombed her hair so that it stood around her head in a huge black cloud. "So do I."

Marnie turned to the side. The shells on her hem clinked like little bells. "I think the costume is sort of cool," she said.

Orla glared. "Not as cool as Gilly's though."

Marnie glanced across the dressing room at the beautiful gown hanging from a peg on the wall. It had

a pale pink sea-moss collar. Pearls studded the bodice.
Pale green and pink sparkles covered the skirt, which was
wide and full and super-swishy. All her life, Marnie had
dreamed of wearing a dress like that.

Eddy swooped up to them, widening his black-lined
eyes. "I am SO ready to get on there and start scowling
and roaring," he said. "You'd better put your makeup on.
We're going on in a minute."

"Ha, ha," said Orla, pulling a gruesome face.

Sighing, Marnie turned back to the mirror and
painted her lips green.

Everyone was gathering in nervous little groups backstage beside the looped pearl curtains. Peeking at the auditorium, Marnie gasped. Every single seat was taken. Fins, scales, and tails glittered in the light from the chandelier. Mermaids swam from box to box, trailing ropes of pearls and long fluffy sea-moss wraps. Marnie glimpsed Christabel in a box close to the stage with her headphones on. Sam was working on the microphones. Sheela was fixing Christabel's hair with a large mother-of-pearl comb as Garbo did somersaults above her head.

Lady Sealia was wearing a gleaming pearl wrap and sitting in the front row with her husband, Lord Foam, a plump merman with a long rust-red beard. Even Dilys had dressed up, wearing a little shell necklace as she dozed on Lady Sealia's shoulders. Ms. Mullet was cracking cockle shells with her claws and chatting with Mr. Splendid, the toadfish stable master. Further back, Marnie glimpsed the waving brown and white fins of Len the lionfish librarian,

and behind him was her mom, looking excited in a very
large pair of blue mussel-shell earrings and her mended
seaweed gown.

"Where is Gilly?" bellowed Miss Tangle. She had
started chewing the ends of her tentacles. "The show is
about to begin!"

The orchestra was starting to tune. Marnie glanced
back at the dressing room. Queen Maretta's beautiful dress
was still hanging on its peg, sparkling in shades of pink
and green.

"Jet's costume is still hanging up too," said Eddy. "I saw it in our dressing room. They're late again. I can't believe it."

"Where do you think they are?" Marnie asked, suddenly feeling worried.

Eddy shrugged. "Who knows?"

"But they're the leads!" Marnie said. "We can't do the show without them."

Miss Tangle gave a little shriek of relief as Gilly and Jet finally appeared. "Oh, thank Neptune! Put on your costumes as quickly as you can, my dears, the show is about to—"

"We've just had the most amazing news!" said Gilly, clasping her hands.

"It's pretty cool," Jet added.

"Yes, yes," said Miss Tangle, trying to herd them toward the dressing room. "You can tell us all about it afterward—"

Gilly gave a little laugh. "Oh, we can't do the show anymore, I'm afraid. We're going to be too busy."

"Yeah," said Jet. "This really cool guy said he can make an album for us."

"And we're going to start recording it **RIGHT AWAY!**" said Gilly. "We need to go straight to his recording

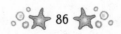

studio. So I'm sorry but obviously we can't do the show now."

"He had an awesome beard," added Jet, stroking his own chin thoughtfully. "Big and blue."

Miss Tangle's eyes bulged. "What?"

"We can't do the show," Gilly repeated.

The music teacher clutched her coral necklace. "What about the audience? What about all our hard work? Who is going to play your parts?"

Gilly shrugged. "I'm sure you understand, Miss Tangle. We were only doing the show to get discovered and now we have been, so there's no point in us doing it. Anyway, we'd rather save our voices for the recording studio. You'll just have to find another queen and prince."

"But . . . this is the *Clamshell Show*!" Miss Tangle spluttered. "Don't you understand how important it is? EVERYONE is here! EVERYONE is watching! Christabel Blue is broadcasting LIVE from the auditorium! You'll never have another chance to perform before this audience again!"

"They can come to our first gig," said Jet. He smirked. "If they can get tickets."

"Bye!" sang Gilly.

And with a flick of their tails, Jet and Gilly swam away.

For a horrible moment, Marnie thought Miss Tangle was going to pop. Out in the auditorium, the chatter was getting louder.

"Are we still going to do the show, Miss Tangle?" asked Dora Agua.

A loud blast from the rock tuba made Miss Tangle jump. She took several deep breaths. "Who knows the part of Prince Cobalt?" she asked.

Eddy raised his hand eagerly. "Me!"

Miss Tangle waved a tentacle at the dressing room. "Change as quickly as you can."

Marnie's head was whirling. Gilly wasn't going to sing the main part anymore. She wasn't going to wear the dress. Miss Tangle was going to—

"Who knows Queen Maretta's part?"

Marnie's hand shot up as fast as an eel from a crevice. So did Orla's.

"We can't have two Queen Marettas," said Miss Tangle helplessly. "One of you will have to let the other one sing it. Make a decision! Quickly!"

Marnie felt like she was in a bad dream. Keeping her hand in the air, she stared at Orla. Orla stared back. It was as if the last few weeks hadn't happened at all.

But then there was a scream from the auditorium that made Marnie forget everything.

"HUMAN! There's a HUMAN in the Clamshell Grotto!"

Arthur hadn't been expecting this. There were mermaids
EVERYWHERE. Half of them were wearing jewels and
fluffy coats. There was an octopus with glasses. There was
even a small dogfish wearing a necklace. He wondered if
he was losing his mind. He couldn't hear anything over
the sound of his oxygen tank.

So he just bobbed in the entrance of the cave and
pulled out his breathing mouthpiece.

"CHRISTABEL!" he shouted, in a burst of
bubbles. "ARE YOU HERE? CHRISTABEL
BLUE?"

Chapter Ten

Marnie couldn't hear anything because of all the screaming. Everyone was rushing out of their seats, swimming as fast as they could past the little figure dressed all in black with a mask on its face and flippers on its feet. A real live human? Here, in the Clamshell Grotto? It was incredible. She looked anxiously for her mom, but couldn't see her.

"Miss Tangle said there's only one way out," gasped Orla, her eyes wide with terror. "This many of us will NEVER fit through one exit. Mermaids are going to get squashed, or we'll get caught by the human!"

Marnie grabbed Orla's hand. "Orla, calm down," she said. "We have to find Lady Sealia. There's another exit somewhere. Lady Sealia told Miss Tangle, but Miss Tangle couldn't remember what it was. Come on!"

Marnie glimpsed a gleaming wrap and necklace in the

middle of the terrified crowds. Lady Sealia seemed to be shouting something about needing her pearls, although that didn't make sense. The headmistress was covered in almost as many pearls as the stage curtains.

The panic was causing a whirlpool, and it was impossible to swim in a straight line. Dilys twirled past uncontrollably. The current was pushing everyone toward the roof of the grotto.

"We'll never reach Lady Sealia against this current," wailed Orla.

Marnie spun around, bumping against the rushing tails and fins of the crowd. *There is another way out,* Miss Tangle had said. *It's only ever used in the face of absolute and total disaster though, or discovery by humans . . .* But where was it? The coral walls loomed on three sides, solid and unbroken by any windows or other doors. There was no way out through the great curved shell that formed the back of the Clamshell Stage either.

Pearl swam up beside Marnie with her hair blowing in a wild red tangle around her head. "I should have tried the lowest notes on the rock tuba when I had the chance," she panted as they fought through the water. "Now we'll never know if they really do make the grotto collapse."

Marnie stared at Pearl, and everything clicked into place.

 93

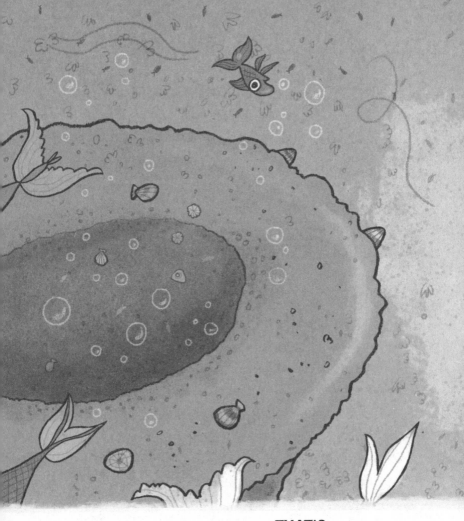

"The rock tuba!" she gasped. "**THAT'S** the other way out! Lady Sealia wasn't saying 'pearls' just now. She was saying 'Pearl.' She needs you to play the rock tuba, Pearl! You play the low notes to open up another exit. Play them as loud as you can!"

Pearl looked excited. "OK! But we'll never get past everyone and back to the rock tuba. It's all the way down there!"

They were above the chandelier now. Phosphorescent fish swam around them in glowing circles. Putting out a

hand to stop herself from banging into the rocky ceiling, Marnie saw what looked like a large, dark cave tucked into a shadowy corner of the roof. She peered inside. It was a tunnel, snaking away and down and out of sight.

"Not **ALL** of the rock tuba is down there," she said suddenly. "Follow me!"

She flipped her tail and dived right into the rock tuba's great stone mouth. *WHOOSH!* Down she went, tumbling through the stony funnel, whizzing and bumping and swooshing along. Up, and around, and along, and down. Faster and faster with Pearl and Orla close behind her.

Marnie shot into the orchestra pit. Orla was next. Pearl was last. Flinging out an arm, Pearl seized one of the rock tuba's stone coils. Pressing her finger to the fattest, lowest limpet button, she pulled herself close to the mouthpiece and blew as hard as she could.

PPPPPRRRRAAₐₐₐₐARRRRRPPPPPP!

There was a thundering creak. Everything shook. Bits of rock fell off the walls and ceiling. The great wavy lips of the Clamshell Stage seemed to tremble.

"More!" screamed Marnie. "MORE!"

Pearl heaved another enormous breath and blew again.

PPPPPRRRRAAAAAAARRRRRPPPPP!

"It's working," shouted Orla.

Veerrry slowly, the mighty Clamshell Stage began to close.

"CHRISTABEL!" Arthur shouted, pulling out his mouthpiece again as he fought through the current. "It's me! It's Arthur!"

Suddenly, she was there, her violet eyes wide and startled. A tiny goldfish darted through her long blonde hair as it blew about in the current. Arthur beamed.

"I've come back," he shouted in a big whoosh of bubbles.

Christabel peered into his mask.

"Blubbering barracudas, Arthur," she said. "Are you out of your mind?"

Chapter Eleven

There was a space behind the Clamshell Stage now, where Marnie could see the dark waters of the lagoon. The top half of the great shell formed the entire back wall of the grotto. As it closed, it provided the perfect way out. Hundreds of mermaids poured through the gap in a flickering shoal and vanished into the night.

"Where's the human?" cried Orla.

A little pink in the face from blowing the rock tuba, Pearl pointed. Marnie frowned. The human was bobbing around in front of Christabel in the *Big Blue Show*'s broadcasting box. It looked like they were actually having a conversation . . .

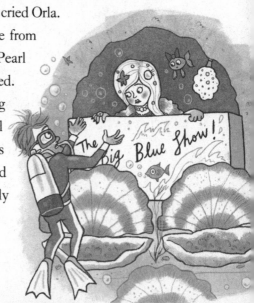

"Please leave, Arthur," Christabel said. "Can't you see how much trouble you've caused?"

"Don't you love me?" Arthur asked, pulling out his mouthpiece. He batted away the goldfish nibbling on his air hose. "These past ten years have been so lonely without you. Don't you feel the same?"

"You know it's impossible," Christabel said. "You're a human and I'm a mermaid!"

"We can work it out," bubbled Arthur with confidence. "There has to be a way."

"We can't even talk to each other properly, Arthur," Christabel pointed out. "Above water, I have no voice. Down here, you can hardly hear me. It's hopeless!"

"But I still love you!" bubbled Arthur.

Garbo hurtled into Marnie's arms as she approached her aunt.

"Are you OK, Aunt Christabel?" Marnie asked, stroking the little goldfish and trying not to stare at the human. Orla and Pearl bobbed a safe distance away.

Christabel pulled a large seaweed handkerchief out of her pocket and wiped her eyes.

"I'm fine, darling," she said.

Marnie peeked at the human again. He looked very odd with his two dangly legs and his weird face mask. What

was he doing here? Why was he talking to Christabel?

"Am I imagining things," said Christabel, "or is the Clamshell Stage closing?"

Marnie blushed. "Remember the rumors about bringing down the whole grotto if you played the low notes on the rock tuba?" she said. "Pearl played the notes."

"It was Marnie's idea," Pearl said.

"Bravo!" Christabel smiled. "You stopped a swimpede!"

"Christabel Blue! I should have known!"

A furious Lady Sealia was swimming across the empty Clamshell Grotto, Dilys clamped under one arm. Her gleaming pearl wrap made a glowing trail behind her. Two mermen with large black beards followed.

Dilys wriggled free and sniffed the human's feet.

"**WHO** is this and **WHAT** is he doing here?" Lady Sealia shrieked.

Christabel sighed.

"This is Arthur, Lady Sealia," she said. "And he was just leaving."

Cuddling Garbo, Marnie exchanged a startled glance with Orla and Pearl.

Arthur?

Arthur was a *human?*

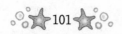

Lady Sealia's eyes narrowed. "How is it possible, Christabel, that you **KNOW** a human?"

Christabel lifted her chin. "We met ten years ago. I told him never to—"

"Our worlds cannot meet!" snapped Lady Sealia. "You know the rules."

"I know. I'm sorry."

"We'll discuss the consequences at another time," Lady Sealia said ominously.

The two mermen grabbed Arthur's arms.

"My husband's guards will escort you to the surface, human," Lady Sealia said. "You may not return. If you try

to, I will curse you. If you ever tell anyone what you saw today, I will send a sea monster to eat you. The Kraken is a close friend."

Arthur spat out his mouthpiece. "I love you, Christabel!" he bubbled as the mermen pulled him away. "I won't give up!"

"Try and forget me, Arthur!" Christabel called after him. "It's for the best!"

"Never!"

"Tragic true love," Pearl sighed when the mermen and Arthur were out of sight. "I told you it was the best kind."

Marnie couldn't see anything good about it at all. All she could see was the way her aunt's eyes had gone red and puffy again. She let go of Garbo and squeezed Christabel's hand.

Lady Sealia raised her voice. "The human has left and will not be coming back. It's safe to come out now!"

A trembling Miss Tangle emerged from a crevice. Ms. Mullet popped up from under one of the sea-moss seats, followed by Mr. Splendid and Mr. Scampi, the lobster oceanography teacher. The Clamshell Show cast and orchestra peeked from behind the pearl curtains. Merfolk began swimming back through the open wall and gathering on top of the shuttered Clamshell Stage. Sam and Sheela came out from behind the chandelier and swam down to the *Big Blue Show*'s broadcasting box.

"A human!" Miss Tangle wailed, wringing her tentacles. "A human found us and will tell the world about us! It's a *catfishtastrophe*!"

"I threatened him with a sea monster if he breathed a word," said Lady Sealia, still glaring at Christabel. "He wouldn't dare."

"But our annual extravaganza is ruined!" Miss Tangle moaned. "All that hard work, for nothing!"

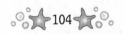

Christabel let go of Marnie's hand. "Don't be silly, Miss Tangle," she said briskly. "Haven't you heard the expression, 'The show must go on'?"

Sam flipped a switch on the *Big Blue Show*'s recording equipment. Christabel leaned in to the large sea-sponge microphone. Her voice traveled around the auditorium and out into the lagoon.

"Good news, Lagooners! The human has left the building and won't be coming back. He was perfectly harmless. Quite handsome too, if I say so myself."

Marnie smiled at Christabel. Her aunt gave her half a smile in return.

"So what are you waiting for?" Christabel continued. "Not even a human can stop the glittering glamour of our annual show. Head on back to Clamshell Grotto and let the magic happen. Curtain up at half past the evening starfish. Stay tuned, tuna fish. We are **BACK**!"

The Last Chapter

"How do we open the stage again, Miss Tangle?" Pearl asked.

"Try the opposite of whatever you did to shut it down," panted Miss Tangle as she rushed past, her tentacles full of driftwood batons. "Backstage, cast! Return to your instruments, orchestra! Quickly!"

The seats were already filling up as Pearl played the highest note on the rock tuba and the Clamshell Stage opened again with a shuddering groan. Everyone applauded as the great curved shell sealed itself back into the wall.

"See you onstage!" said Eddy, hurrying past Marnie in Prince Cobalt's blue and gold costume.

They still hadn't decided who was going to play Queen Maretta yet. Marnie raced to the dressing room.

Orla was waiting beside the sparkly pink-and-green

dress. As they stared at each other, Marnie thought about Christabel's puffy eyes and the difficult choice that her aunt had made. She didn't want to choose between her friend and her singing. Not now.

"You can play Queen Maretta if you want," she said.

"I think you should play Queen Maretta," Orla said at the same time.

Marnie blinked. "Leaping lobsters," she said. "Really?"

Orla's cheeks turned pink. "I was thinking about what was important when everyone was panicking and no one knew how to get out," she said. "The way you worked out the thing about the rock tuba, and how you shut the Clamshell Stage and saved everyone from squishing each other . . . You're *important*, Marnie. And you deserve the part. I'm sorry I've been so horrible about it."

Marnie felt a great weight lift off her shoulders. "Let's share it," she said. "You sing the first half and I'll sing the second."

"You mean it?" Orla gasped.

Marnie laughed. "Queen Maretta gets an even better dress after the interval."

"You're the best, Marnie!" Orla squealed.

"No," Marnie said, hugging her best friend tightly. "WE'RE the best."

Marnie wanted to hold on to every moment. Everything was magical. Exactly as she'd always imagined. Algie's beautiful razor-clam flute duet with the coral clarinets. The stomping, shouting storm sprites. Orla in the

pink and green dress. And in the second act, Marnie wore blue and gold and twirled around the stage with Prince Cobalt in the grand finale, singing and meaning every word.

"The song of the sea, for you and for me,
The love in the air that all of us share,
A storm is a gift, the sea needs a change,
The seasons will shift, it isn't so strange,
Storm sprites and merfolk must now make amends,
Let's sing and let's dance and let's always be friends.
Let's al-ways be friends!"

The audience threw sea roses that drifted onto the stage. And the whole auditorium echoed with cheers and applause as Marnie and Eddy took their bow together.

After the show, the compliments flowed like seaweed in a strong current. Marnie smoothed down her blue and gold dress and shook hands and smiled until her face hurt. Right beside her, Orla was doing the same. Miss Tangle was shaking eight hands at a time.

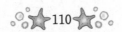

"Good work, your majesties," said Eddy with a silly bow.

"You too, Eddy!" said Marnie happily.

"Thrills and gills, Marnie, you did great!" Marnie's mom had lost one of her mussel earrings and her face was pink with excitement. "I'm as proud as a pufferfish!"

"Thanks, Mom," said Marnie, hugging her tightly.

"Marvelous work. Really wonderful." A mermaid with a thick rope of black pearls twisted through her ebony hair was smiling at Marnie and Orla. "I'm Lavinia Freshwater," she said. "Excellent teamwork tonight."

Feeling a little dazed, Marnie shook the hand of one of the most famous music agents in Mermaid Lagoon.

"Thank you, Ms. Freshwater," she stammered. "I'm Marnie Blue, and this is my friend, Orla Finnegan."

"Any time you or Orla need advice, Marnie, send me a scallop," Lavinia said. "You both have a great future ahead of you."

"Neptune's knickers," Orla said as Lavinia Freshwater swam away. "Did that just happen?"

Christabel beamed. "Well done, darlings." Garbo darted around in flickering gold loops as Christabel hugged Marnie and Orla. "Lavinia Freshwater is very hard to impress."

Marnie suddenly saw Gilly and Jet huddled beside the pearl curtains with Lady Sealia.

"SUCH a shame you didn't sing tonight," Lady Sealia was saying as she stroked Dilys's whiskers. "Lavinia Freshwater was MOST disappointed not to hear you."

"Why aren't those two off recording their album?" Pearl said, swimming over with a glass of sparkling seawater.

Sheela put her arm around Orla's waist. "Probably because there IS no album."

"What?" said Orla and Marnie at the same time.

Sheela grinned. "It was a test. Flip and I set it up."

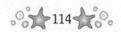

She waved across the stage at Flip. He waved back, his gold tooth flashing through his blue beard.

Marnie gaped at Sheela. "So it was *Flip* I saw Gilly and Jet talking to in that box?"

"There was no recording contract?" Pearl said.

"You tricked them?" said Orla.

"They tricked themselves," Sheela said. "Flip only told them that he could record an album for them—which is technically true. They imagined the rest. Gilly and Jet didn't **HAVE** to abandon the show. They **CHOSE** to."

"Why did you do it?" asked Pearl.

Sheela shrugged. "They needed to learn a lesson about fame the hard way. And they annoyed me."

Orla laughed and Marnie decided then and there never to annoy Sheela Finnegan.

"That's him!" Gilly's wail rose over the chatter. She pointed at Flip. "That's the guy! He said he'd record an album for us but no one was at the studio and now everything's gone wrong!"

Lady Sealia sighed. "Dilys was SO looking forward to hearing you. Now we have to wait until next year's Clamshell Show."

A song blasted out across the grotto. All the party guests stopped chatting and started wiggling to the music. Pearl zoomed past with Algie. Eddy twirled with Orla. Marnie's mom was dancing very carefully with Len the librarian. Ms. Mullet and Mr. Scampi scuttled past, doing some kind of shellfish tango.

But Christabel was at the side of the stage, stroking the pearl curtains with a faraway look on her face. It wasn't hard to guess what she was thinking about.

"Are you OK?" Marnie asked, swimming over.

Christabel lifted her elegant shoulders. "I chose my life in Mermaid Lagoon ten years ago. I couldn't leave

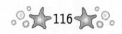

you all behind then, and I can't leave you behind now.
So until we work out how a human and a mermaid can be
together, I'll have to be OK about Arthur."

"And what about Lady Sealia?" asked Marnie.

Christabel snorted.

"She doesn't scare me! Everything will be fine, Marnie.
Don't you worry."

Marnie looked up at her aunt and smiled. "You're
amazing."

Christabel tossed her long blonde hair. "Tell me
something I don't know, shrimp." She grinned. "And
you're pretty special yourself."

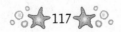

Offishially The Last Chapter

The mermen escorted Arthur most of the way back to the surface. Arthur thought about fighting them off and swimming back, but they looked pretty strong. There was also the small matter of the curse . . .

Thoughts of a sea monster biting his feet made Arthur swim the last few feet to the boat extremely fast. He spluttered and coughed as the first mate pulled him aboard. His air tank was almost out of oxygen. He lay on the deck, breathing deeply and enjoying the sun on his face.

"Anything down there?"

Large violet eyes, Arthur thought. *Long blonde hair.*

"Perhaps," he said.

"Worth another look?" asked the first mate.

Arthur sighed. "Let's go home for now."

FIN

About the Author

Lucy Courtenay has worked on a number of series for young readers, as well as books for young adults. When not writing, she enjoys singing, reading, and traveling. She lives in Farnham, England, with her husband, her two sons, and a cat named Crumbles.

About the Illustrator

Sheena Dempsey is a children's book illustrator and author from Cork, Ireland, who was shortlisted for the Sainsbury's Book Award. She lives in London with her partner, Mick, and her retired racing greyhound, Sandy.